Usborne
# Build your own
# DEADLY
# ANIMALS
## Sticker Book

Designed by Reuben Barrance and Marc Maynard
Written by Simon Tudhope

Illustrated by Franco Tempesta

Consultants: Dr. Margaret Rostron and Dr. John Rostron

## Contents

# Bengal tiger

This solitary hunter prowls through the night. And now, as the sun begins to rise, it finds its moment to strike. Bursting from the forest in a blur of gold, it drags its prey to the ground.

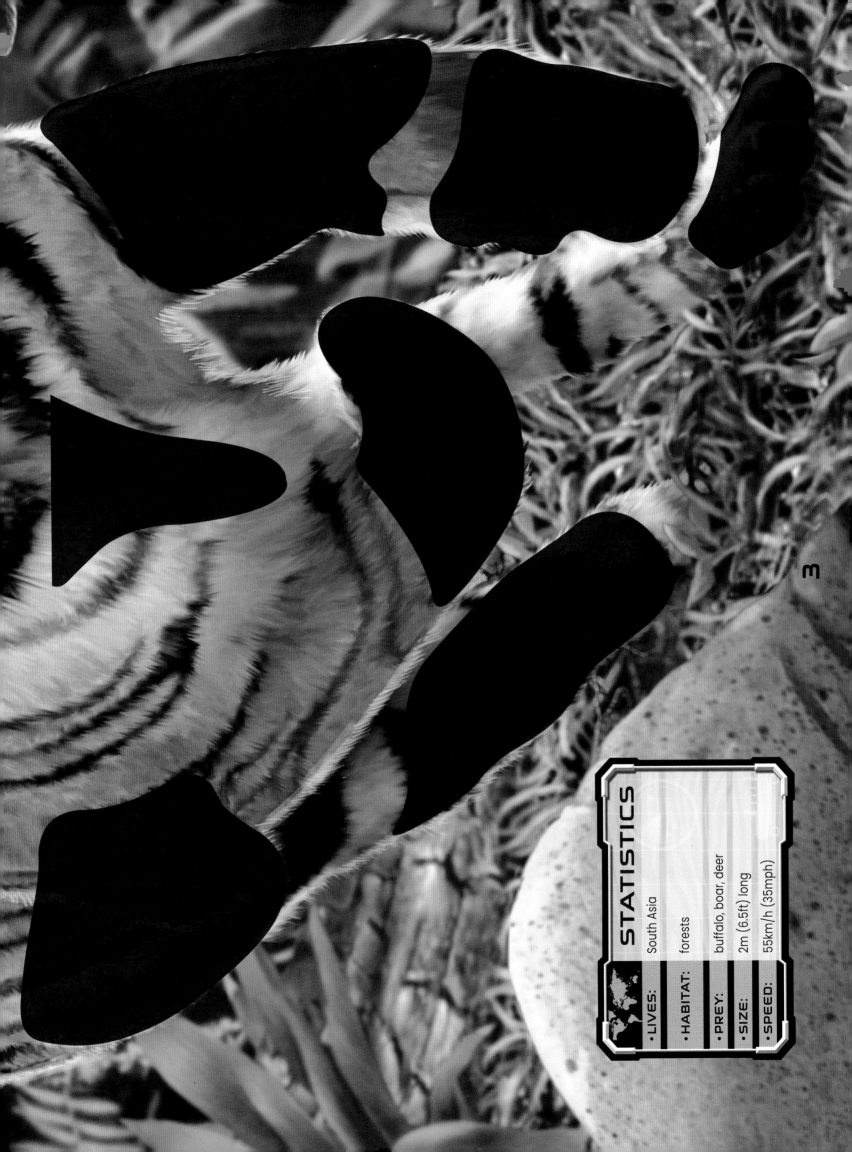

3

## STATISTICS

| | |
|---|---|
| •LIVES: | South Asia |
| •HABITAT: | forests |
| •PREY: | buffalo, boar, deer |
| •SIZE: | 2m (6.5ft) long |
| •SPEED: | 55km/h (35mph) |

# King cobra

Meet the largest venomous snake on the planet. It rears up, high enough to look a person in the eye, and flares its hood. Behind those fangs is enough venom to kill an elephant. With a low, growling hiss, it waits for the intruder to back away.

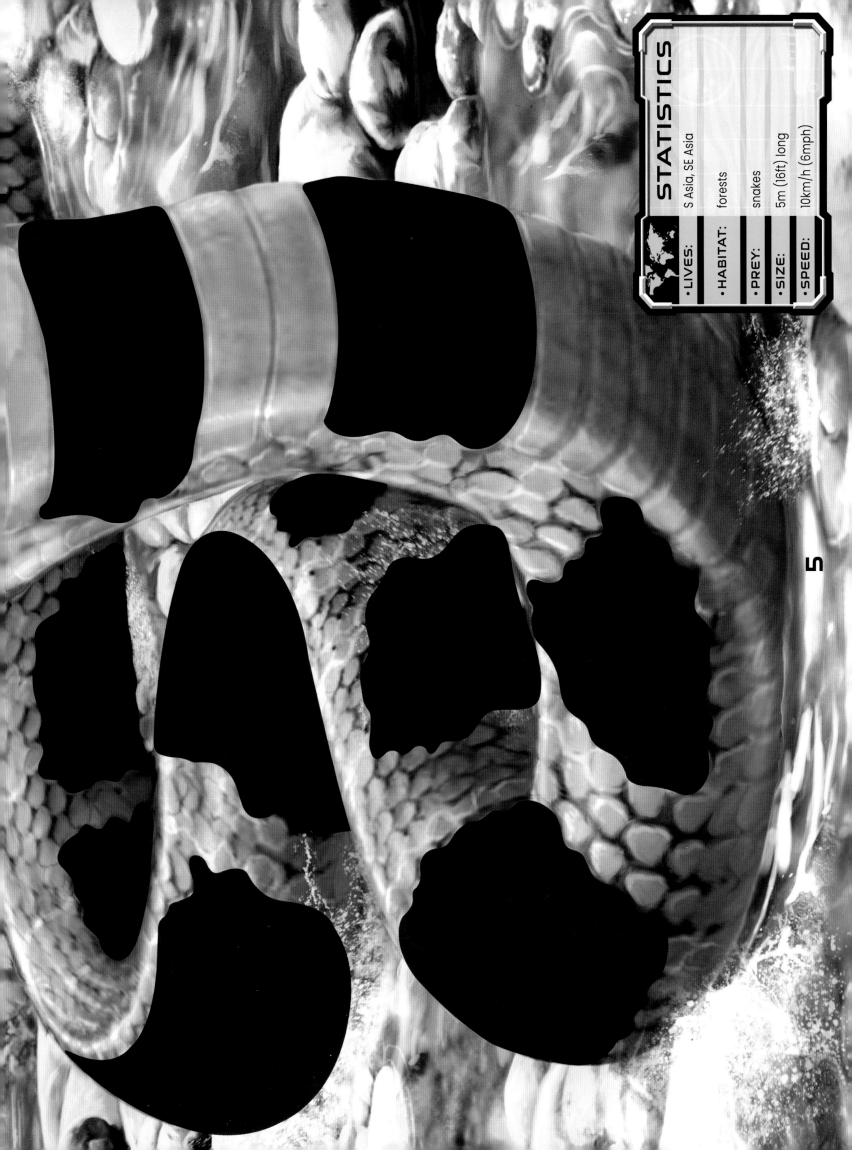

**STATISTICS**

- LIVES: S Asia, SE Asia
- HABITAT: forests
- PREY: snakes
- SIZE: 5m (16ft) long
- SPEED: 10km/h (6mph)

# Giant squid

In the cold ocean depths swims a creature with
eyes the size of dinner plates. Its tentacles snake
forwards out of the gloom, and at their base,
a hooked beak emerges. Strong enough
to bite through a bullet-proof vest, it waits
for the tentacles to deliver their catch.

## STATISTICS

| | |
|---|---|
| • LIVES: | temperate oceans |
| • HABITAT: | deep ocean |
| • PREY: | deep-sea fish, squid |
| • SIZE: | 13m (43ft) long |
| • SPEED: | not known |

# Saltwater crocodile

This ambush predator has the most powerful bite of any creature on Earth. And once those jaws lock on, nothing escapes – not even buffalo. That fish doesn't stand a chance...

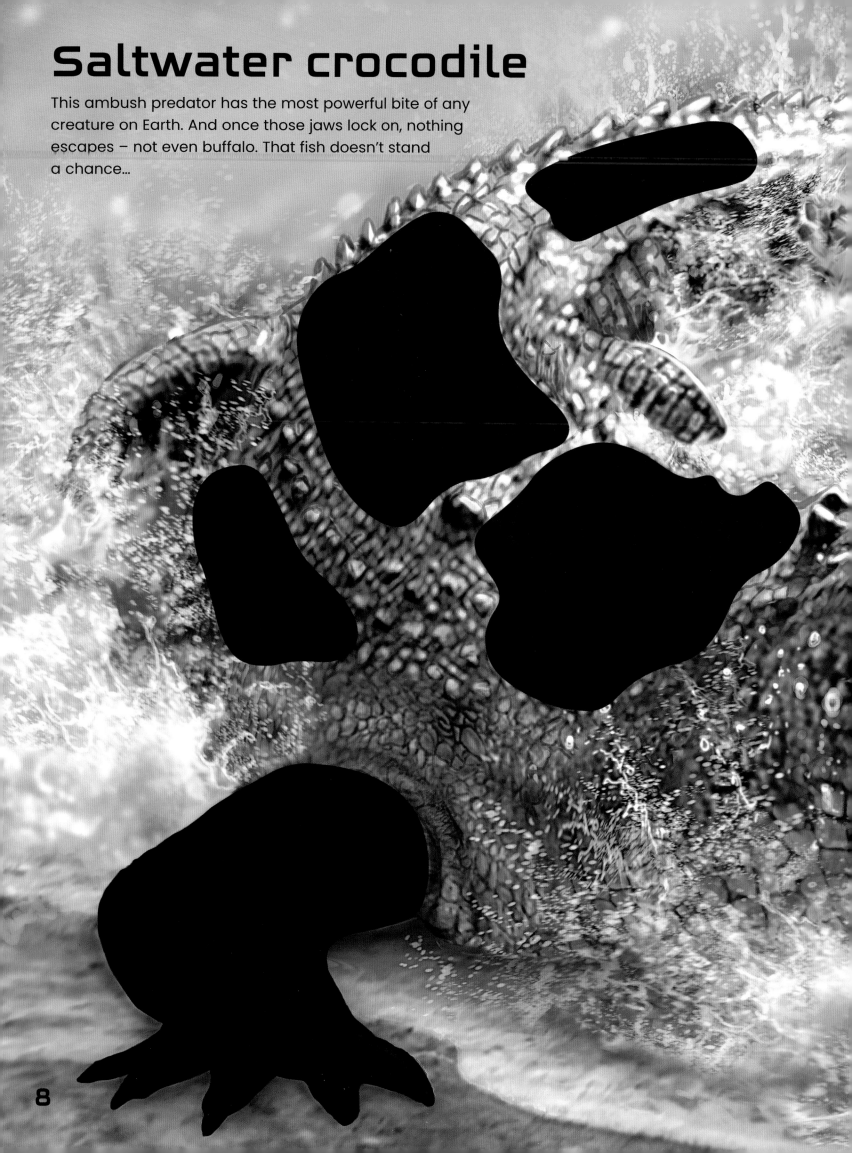

# Great white shark

Perhaps the world's ultimate hunter. It can smell a drop
of blood from a quarter of a mile away, and pinpoints
its prey from the beating of its heart.

## STATISTICS

| | |
|---|---|
| •LIVES: | temperate oceans |
| •HABITAT: | coastal waters |
| •PREY: | fish, seals, sharks, dolphins |
| •SIZE: | 6m (20ft) long |
| •SPEED: | 25km/h (16mph) |

# Asian giant hornet

You hear them before you see them, the drone drowning out the sounds of the forest. They've come to feast on honey bees – thousands of them. Just thirty of these giant hornets can wipe out a hive that's thirty-thousand strong.

**STATISTICS**

| | |
|---|---|
| •LIVES: | E Asia, SE Asia |
| •HABITAT: | forests, low mountains |
| •PREY: | bees, beetles, mantises |
| •SIZE: | 4cm (1.6in) long |
| •SPEED: | 40km/h (25mph) |

# Wolf

The howls roll down the icy cliffs – a warning
that the valley below belongs to the wolves.
They're the top predators here, hunting
as a pack to bring even the biggest
animal to its knees.

## STATISTICS

| | |
|---|---|
| •LIVES: | N America, Asia, Europe |
| •HABITAT: | forests, grasslands, mountains, deserts |
| •PREY: | elk, deer, bison |
| •SIZE: | 1.5m (5ft) long |
| •SPEED: | 65km/h (40mph) |

# Indian red scorpion

The world's most deadly scorpion has a cockroach in its grip. The stinger hangs poised, then whips down one, two, three times. It doesn't take long for the venom to do its work.

17

# Peregrine falcon

The fastest animal ever. Folding back its wings and diving towards its prey, it reaches speeds of over 200mph. Flashing past skyscrapers, mountains or coastal cliffs, it rules the skies wherever it lives.

## STATISTICS

| | |
|---|---|
| •LIVES: | all continents except Antarctica |
| •HABITAT: | everywhere except polar regions and tropical rainforests |
| •PREY: | birds |
| •SIZE: | 1m (40in) wingspan |
| •SPEED: | 389km/h (242mph) |

# Brazilian wandering spider

This silent hunter picks its way through the jungle night. Armed with one of the most venomous bites of any spider, it likes to feast on lizards and mice.

## STATISTICS

| | |
|---|---|
| • LIVES: | S America, Central America |
| • HABITAT: | rainforests |
| • PREY: | insects, lizards, mice |
| • SIZE: | 18cm (7in) legspan |
| • SPEED: | less than 1km/h (0.6mph) |

# Lion

In one of the most fiercely contested habitats on the planet, this beast is king. It bands together with other lions to form formidable fighting units that dominate the African plains.

# Glossary

- **DRONE:** a low, continuous noise

- **HABITAT:** an animal's natural environment

- **HIVE:** a group of bees that live together in a nest made from honeycombs

- **HUMID:** weather that's hot and sticky

- **PACK:** a group of animals that live and hunt together

- **PREDATOR:** an animal that hunts

- **PREY:** an animal that's hunted

- **TEMPERATE:** a temperate ocean is neither as warm as a tropical ocean, nor as cold as a polar ocean

- **VENOM:** poison produced by animals and injected by biting or stinging

Edited by Sam Taplin

Digital manipulation by Keith Furnival

First published in 2021 by Usborne Publishing Limited, 83-85 Saffron Hill, London EC1N 8RT, United Kingdom. usborne.com

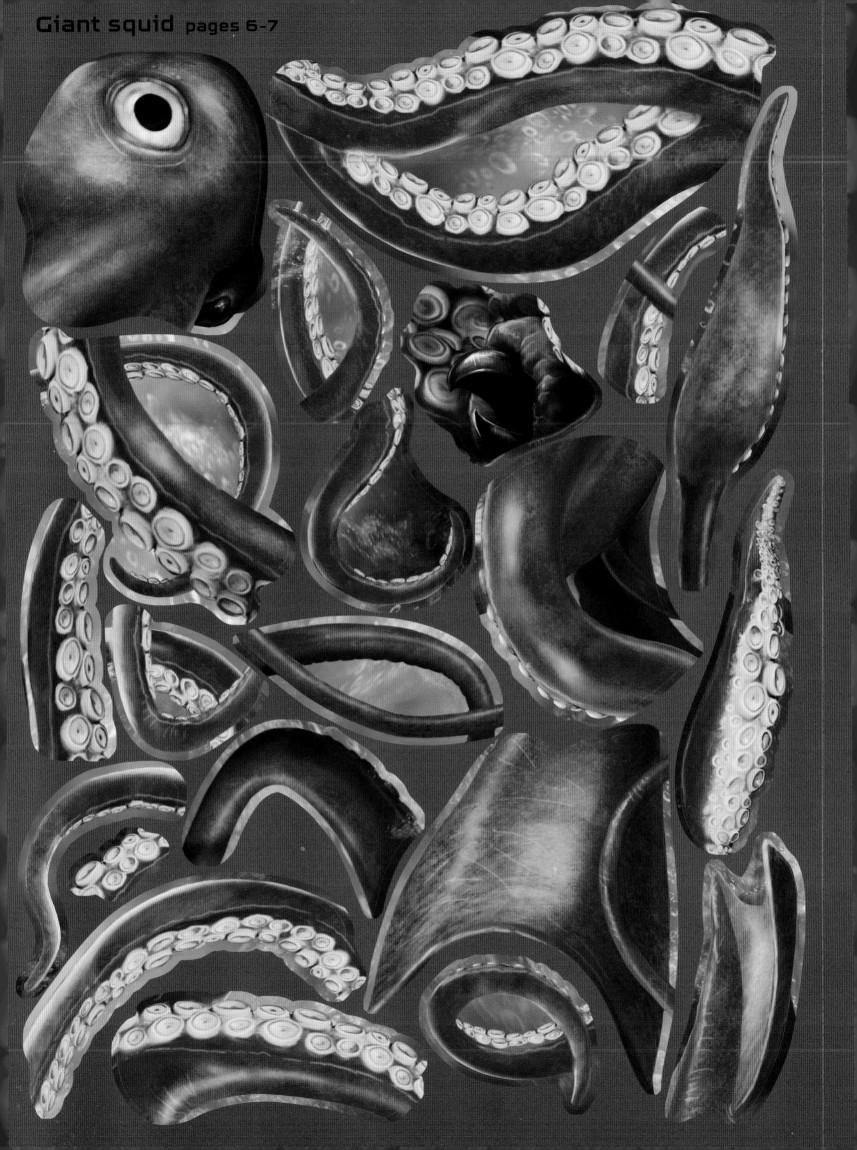

## Lion pages 22-23